What's Bugging Carter?
Junior Medical Detective Series
Volume 2

Ali Raja, Vanisha Gilja Shah, and Kaushal Shah

Guest Author
Jonathan Edlow, MD

Illustrated by
Mel Casipit

To our families, for their love and support.

It's a beautiful, warm summer evening, and Chase and his little brother Carter are playing frisbee. The sun is starting to set and Chase's mom calls for them. "Come on in, boys! It's time for dinner and your dad and I want to talk to you about something."

Chase's dad asks, "What do you think about taking a week long camping trip? You boys have never been to the White Mountains in New Hampshire." Chase and Carter shout "Yippee!".

Chase is really excited. "Can we invite Naya? Can we? Can we?" Chase's Dad chuckles. "Sure, why not? Let me call Naya's parents to ask if they'd like to join us."

Naya can't sit still in the car because she's too excited. "Are we there yet? I can't wait to see my friends and go camping." says Naya. Naya's mom smiles and replies "For the hundredth time, we'll be at the campsite very soon."

"Ok, ok. Did you pack the cupcakes I made?" says Naya. Naya's mom replies, "Yes, honey. But you know packing the sunscreen and water are more important than the cupcakes, right?" Naya is still thinking about cupcakes.

While the kids give each other high fives, their moms are trying to get sunscreen on everyone!

"What a beautiful day for a hike. When do we stop for lunch?" asks Chase. Carter shouts, "Never! Let's keep going. I think we're almost to the top of the mountain."

Carter runs ahead and slips, striking his knee. "You ok, Carter?" asks Naya. "Yup, solid as a rock!" He brushes off his knee and rushes ahead.

"Thanks for the sandwiches, Mom" says Chase.
"Yeah, thanks, Mom!" adds Carter. "Drink more water, everyone!" their mom replies.
They spend the next week exploring trails, picking flowers, collecting rocks and swimming.

The gang sits around the fire, roasting marshmallows, making s'mores and telling scary stories. Naya comments, "I can't believe the week is over and it's our last night of camping."

The next day, Chase sees Carter holding his head.
"What's wrong?" he asks. "My head hurts." Carter
replies.
"Oh, Carter," says his dad, "you've probably just been out
in the sun too long. Here – have some water."

"Hey, do you see that redness on the back of Carter's leg? I want to take a closer look." Naya pulls out a magnifying glass from her backpack.

"It's just a bruise from the hiking. Put some ice on it," says his Mom. Chase and Naya are not convinced. Naya remembers that he fell on the front of his knee. Chase asks Naya, "How could he get a bruise on the back of his leg if he fell on his kneecap?"

Naya pokes the red area and says "Does it hurt?"
"Nope!" replies Carter. Chase says, "Wait a sec!
Bruises usually hurt. There are no scratches and it's
not purple like all of the bruises I've seen before".
Chase puts ice on Carter's leg anyway.

His mom says, "You must have fallen a lot this week. We still have a long way to go. Let me carry you for a little while."

Chase takes another look at Carter's leg. The red area has become bigger. "I put ice on it so the bruise shouldn't have gotten bigger. This looks like a "bull's eye!"".

Naya tugs on her Dad's sleeve. "I really think we should have a doctor look at Carter. I don't think he has a bruise on his leg. It doesn't hurt and the red area is getting bigger and bigger. Carter usually has so much energy and now he's feeling tired and achy." "Good thinking, Naya. I think you're right. Let's go."

"Hi everyone, I'm Dr. Edlow. What seems to be the problem?" Chase points to the red mark on Carter's leg.

"So you have a headache, you feel tired and achy, and now you have this rash?" Carter nods. Have you been outside hiking recently?" "Yes!" replies Carter. "I just went camping in the White Mountains for a week."

"I think you have Lyme disease," says Dr. Edlow. "You probably got bitten by a bug called a tick that caused the bull's eye rash on your leg." Carter replies in disbelief, "I don't remember being bitten by anything." Dr. Edlow explains "A person who gets bitten by a tick usually won't feel anything at all. Ticks are very small and can be hard to see. And symptoms don't appear until several days or even weeks after you've been bitten."

Edlow continues, "There are no guaranteed ways to avoid Lyme Disease, but there are ways to be more careful. If you are in an area that is known to have ticks, wear long sleeves, long pants and shoes that cover your toes. Use bug spray whenever you use sunscreen. Most importantly, check your body for ticks regularly. You can ask a parent to help you with a nightly tick check as part of your bedtime routine."

"Many people ignore the symptoms of Lyme disease," says Nurse Linda. "Chase and Naya were very smart to realize that you needed to see a doctor." Dr. Edlow says, "We can start you on a type of medicine called an antibiotic. We will have you feeling better in no time!"

Everyone is relieved. Naya's mom says, "Great job kids! We are very proud of you". Naya replies, "Thanks, Mom. Are there any cupcakes left?" Everyone laughs.

Circle the five items that you need to be safe on a camping trip:

Despite its name, Lyme Disease actually has nothing to do with limes. You can get Lyme Disease if you are bitten by a tiny bug called a tick. It is common for a "bull's eye" rash to appear on the skin at the sight of the tick bite. Some ticks carry bacteria called spirochetes (spy-ruh-keets). If these get inside of a person, they may get Lyme Disease. However, Lyme Disease can be easily treated with a type of medicine called an antibiotic!

What's Bugging Carter?

Junior Medical Detective Series
Volume 2

Ali Raja is an emergency physician in Boston.   His son Carter has never had Lyme disease but, if he gets it, Ali and his wife Danielle hope that his older brother Chase is able to diagnose it.

Vanisha Gilja Shah holds a double Masters in Counseling Psychology and Organizational Psychology from Teachers College, Columbia University. She has over 10 years of experience working with children in educational and medical settings. Vanisha lives in Manhasset, NY with her husband, and their two very own junior medical detectives, Naya and Mila.

Kaushal Shah is an emergency physician in NYC who believes there is a medical detective in all of us -- you just have to learn to see the clues.   He lives on Long Island with his wife, Vanisha, and their two mischievous daughters.

Jonathan Edlow is an emergency physician in Massachusetts who has always been fascinated by ticks and tick-borne diseases. He has written 2 books, one about the history of Lyme disease (Bull's Eye) and another collection of true medical detective stories (The Deadly Dinner Party).

30208428R00018

Made in the USA
Middletown, DE
16 March 2016